KT-557-162

25 p.

ZOLDO THE MAGNIFICENT

Kites

TAKE OFF WITH A KITE!

This lively series is designed for children who have developed reading fluency and enjoy reading complete books on their own.

The stories are attractively presented with plenty of illustrations which make them satisfying and fun! A perfect follow-on from the Read Alone series.

ROBIN KINGSLAND

ZOLDO THE MAGNIFICENT

VIKING

VIKING

Published by the Penguin Group
Penguin Books Ltd, 27 Wrights Lane, London W8 5TZ, England
Penguin Books USA Inc., 375 Hudson Street, New York, New York 10014, USA
Penguin Books Australia Ltd, Ringwood, Victoria, Australia
Penguin Books Canada Ltd, 10 Alcorn Avenue, Toronto, Ontario, Canada
M4V 3B2
Penguin Books (NZ) Ltd, 182–190 Wairau Road, Auckland 10, New Zealand

Penguin Books Ltd, Registered Offices: Harmondsworth, Middlesex, England

First published 1993
10 9 8 7 6 5 4 3 2 1

Text and illustration copyright © Robin Kingsland, 1993

The moral right of the author/illustrator has been asserted

Filmset in Linotron Palatino 14/22 pt by
Rowland Phototypesetting Ltd, Bury St Edmunds, Suffolk
Printed in Great Britain by
Butler and Tanner Ltd, Frome and London

A CIP catalogue record for this book is available from the British Library

ISBN 0–670–83600–1

L7 06471199

RO
/5F/C

ONE

This is the story of a hat.

Actually it's the story of a hat . . . and two men . . . and a couple of doves . . . and a dog . . . and some jewels and a holiday.

But mostly, it's about a hat.

I know what you're thinking.

You're thinking: "Oh, no! I've just spent good money on this book and it turns out to be about a hat! A *hat* for goodness' sake!"

All I can say is that this is no ordinary hat, for it belongs to none other than

I know what you're thinking.

You're thinking: "Who's Windrush Gussett when he's at home?"

Perhaps I'd better explain.

TWO

When Windrush Gussett is at home, he is . . . well, he's just Windrush Gussett really. He makes tea . . .

and cuts his toenails . . .

and digs the garden like anybody else.

It's when he's *not* at home that he's different, because if he's *not* at home the

chances are that Windrush Gussett is
dazzling audiences using his other
name – which is:

You must have heard of Zoldo. Zoldo
the Magnificent is famous all over the
world. He does magic.

When Windrush was still very small, he
revealed an amazing talent . . .

By the time he was six relatives were
queuing up to be sawn in half by him.
As soon as he left school he bought . . .

a second-hand magic wand,

a second-hand hat,

two second-hand doves,

That's us!

FRED   GINGER

a battered old second-hand suitcase,

and became

Things went well for Zoldo, and then one day, an old magician told Zoldo the legend of the Mysterious Hat Man.

But Zoldo believed it.

THREE

In the remotest corner of the
Bramazonian rain forest is a village of
tiny huts, and it was in the remotest hut
of this remote village that Zoldo first
made the acquaintance of the Legendary
Hat Man!

Zoldo knocked on the rough wooden door and went in.

"Ah, come in, sit down," said the Hat Man. "See anything you like?"

(The Hat Man, by the way, did have a name, but you probably couldn't pronounce it and I certainly couldn't spell it, so we'll just call him "The Hat Man" and leave it at that.)

The Hat Man had been making hats all his life. His father had made them before him, and *his* father had made them before him, and *his* father . . .

well, you get the idea.

Zoldo looked around at all the hundreds of hats on display. He nodded and smiled at the Hat Man, feeling a bit awkward. Then he suddenly blurted out: "Can I have one of your magic hats please!"

The Hat Man looked up from his work. "That depends," he said.

You see, the magic hats were made from a special pattern, using rare threads and materials. There were no tricks, no flaps and no false bottoms. These hats contained magic. Real magic. Pure and simple. But, because this made the hats awesomely powerful, the Hat Man was very careful about who he made them for. They had to be good magicians and they had to be good people.

Zoldo showed the Hat Man every trick he knew.

The Hat Man  didn't clap. He
didn't smile. He simply sat
cross-legged on the floor
for a long time and
looked at Zoldo.

Zoldo began to worry. Had he upset the
Hat Man? Maybe his tricks weren't good
enough? Zoldo held his breath. Then, at
long last, the Hat Man got up.

We had better measure your head, Mr Zoldo. It wouldn't do if your hat were too small.

That was how Zoldo acquired his magic hat. It was his most prized possession. He never let it out of his sight. He hardly ever took it off.

But even the magic hat could not save Zoldo on . . .

FOUR

The Night When It All Went Horribly
Wrong started off normally enough.
Zoldo was feeling a little

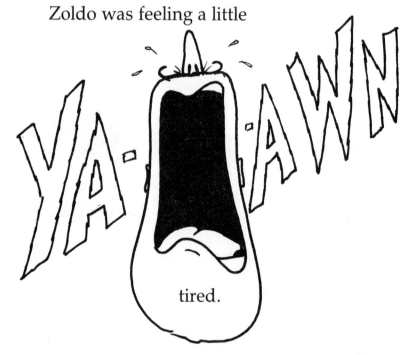

tired.

That was all.

Zoldo strode on to the stage.
Everybody cheered like mad.

Zoldo bowed. Everybody cheered
again. Things, as usual, were going
brilliantly. And then, all of a sudden, in

the middle of his producing-handful-after-handful-of-playing-cards trick, Zoldo felt an odd feeling at the back of his jaw. A sort of a dull tickle that got worse and worse until . . .

right there . . .

in front
of thousands
of people . . .

Zoldo had never felt this way before. His eyes began to droop and his head nodded forward. He just could not concentrate. When the King of Hearts was supposed to rise magically from the pack, nothing happened. Zoldo tapped

the pack harder with his wand . . . still
nothing. He tapped even harder. It half
worked. The King of Hearts didn't rise
up . . .

but all
the rest of
the
cards

fell

down . . .

BOO!

RUBBISH!

Things went very quickly down
hill.

Zoldo's trained doves were worried about him.

I'm worried, Ginger. Me too, Fred.

Zoldo's performance had turned into a shambles. The stage was awash with wreckage.

The nightmare only ended when, to the sound of boos, he bowed weakly and shuffled off.

FIVE

"I don't understand it," said Zoldo in the dressing-room. "None of those tricks has gone wrong before!"

"You're tired," Ginger said. "I was saying to Fred 'He's tired', wasn't I, Fred?"

"It's true," said Fred. "You look terrible."

Zoldo went over to the mirror.

Fred and Ginger were right.

Zoldo was not the only person having a bad night that night. A couple of miles away, Milo Drumgooey was not doing well either.

Milo was a jewel thief.

This is Milo . . . the one without the fur. The other one is Fang.

In his time, Milo had been one of the best jewel thieves in the business – or worst, if you see what I mean – but lately he'd been having a run of bad luck.

For example, on his burglars "crime-a-day" year planner for this particular night, Milo had written:

But when he got to Gosport Road, he tried to get into Number 29 by mistake.

So while he was
trying to find the
diamond bracelet
which should
have been there
but wasn't,

Milo set off a burglar alarm,

which shouldn't have been there but
was, and had to spend the entire night in
a tree hiding from the police . . .

who were everywhere!

I think I should go away for a little bit, Milo decided, before they put me away for a *big* bit.

SIX

Two days later all the holiday arrangements were complete, and a smiling, excited Zoldo took his place in the queue at the bus stop.

Then he took his place
in the queue at the
railway station . . .

and the
airport.

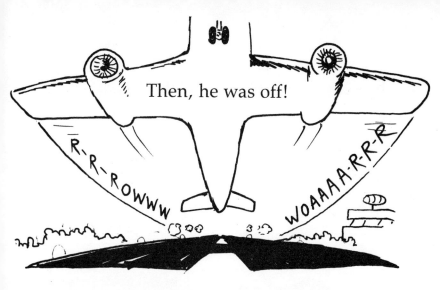

Then, he was off!

Zoldo the Magnificent put his seat
back as far as it would go. Then, using
no magic whatsoever, he turned himself
into Windrush Gussett . . . and went to
sleep.

Saint Oriel was a tropical paradise, full of beaches and posh hotels. But hotels didn't bother Windrush. He had the sun, the sea, sandy beaches and long, cool drinks.

The hotels didn't bother Milo Drumgooey either:

Already looking round to select his
first victim, Milo went up to the
reception desk to get his room key.
But . . .

Milo was hopping mad.

SEVEN

Windrush Gussett spent several days of
his holiday relaxing. But he still wore
that hat everywhere.

"You'd get more sun on you if you took your hat off," said Fred, but Windrush wouldn't hear of it.

Ginger tried. "But while you're here, you're not Zoldo any more. You're Windrush. Windrush doesn't need the hat!"

Still Windrush shook his head.

"The powers of this hat are so amazing," he said, "I just can't afford to let it out of my sight. It can make things appear, disappear, reappear! Suppose it got into the wrong hands!" Windrush shivered. "Or on to the wrong head!

It's too dreadful to even _think_ about!

Little did Zoldo know that the wrong hands and the wrong head were listening to every word from a nearby table.

Back at the pool-side, Ginger had a suggestion. "Why don't you leave your hat in the hotel room?" she asked.

"Yes. In a box," said Fred.

"In the room, in a box, on the wardrobe," Ginger added. "No one would know it was there. It would be quite safe."

Zoldo thought.

So, later that day . . .

EIGHT

A daring daylight raid is about to take place . . .

SPLUK!

SPLOK!

51

The manager of the Bay Vistas Hotel had the sort of face that looked worried even if nothing was wrong. And right now, things were terribly, terribly wrong.

The manager looked

PANIC STRICKEN!

All morning, his richest guests had been crammed in his tiny office, all screaming that their jewellery was gone and what was he going to do about it. He tried to keep everybody calm while he took descriptions of the suspected thieves. They were all different. The thief was either . . .

short, with a patch
over one eye . . .

short with a beard
and glasses . . .

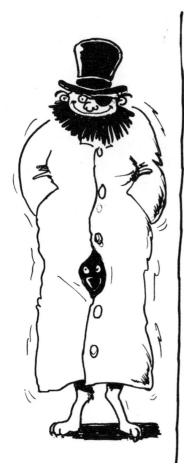 

tall with a beard
and a patch over
one eye . . .

or tall with
smelly breath
and pointy ears.

All the suspects had one thing in
common though . . .

"And how exactly," the manager asked, "did this person steal your valuables?"

Nobody knew for sure. This top-hatted person would come up to them by the pool, or on the beach, lift his hat politely, whisper something that sounded like "Abracadabra", and then run. It wasn't until he'd gone that anyone noticed their jewellery missing.

The manager made an announcement.

The people did what people do when other people tell them not to panic . . .

The manager crawled to the phone and asked for the police.

I know what you're thinking.

You're thinking: "Where is Windrush Gussett all this time?"

Well, Windrush Gussett, along with Fred and Ginger, had been on a day trip organized by the hotel. They had been to see an old castle, had a meal in a nice café and been to see how prunes are made. When he got back, Windrush was planning to have a drink by the pool and a lie-down before supper . . .

He was not planning to be arrested for the daylight robbery of everybody's jewels.

Only one person was happy that night.

"I think we'll lie low for a bit," Milo said. "Don't want to be too conspicuous, do I?"

At the local gaol, Windrush Gussett was being interviewed by the police chief.

It took a long time, but in the end they managed to convince the police that neither Zoldo *nor* Windrush Gussett had been around when the robberies took place.

"This is all very well, Señor Gussett," said the police chief, "but the fact remains that a crime has been committed, and we think your hat is at the bottom of it."

"Perhaps if we work together, we can catch the real criminal!" Windrush said.

NINE

The hotel manager was very apologetic.

"Ah, Señor Gussett! Forgive me. When I heard the man wore a top hat . . ."

"I understand," Zoldo said. "The main thing now is, how do we catch the person who stole the jewels . . . and my hat?"

Everybody racked their brains for an idea. The police had been combing the area all day, but since the alarm had been raised, no one had seen a man in a top hat anywhere.

Fred and Ginger were particularly keen to come up with a plan. They felt that the whole horrible business was their fault to begin with. They went off together and thought . . .

and thought . . .

and thought.

Then suddenly . . .

Fred and Ginger flapped and fluttered
back to the hotel to find everyone else.
And when the others heard Fred and
Ginger's plan they said:

Next day, posters appeared all over town:

TONIGHT!
FANCY DRESS
TOP HAT PARTY
(NO TOP HAT — NO ENTRY!)
~now~
Special Appearance by
ZOLDO
the Magnificent!

I know what you're thinking.

You're thinking: "Oh, no! If everyone is going to wear a top hat, then Milo will be able to rob people left, right and centre, and they'll never even know!"

Of course you are right. And that is exactly what Milo Drumgooey was supposed to think, too.

TEN

Milo and Fang stole some fancy clothes from a costume shop, and got ready for the party.

"All them posh people will be there," chuckled Milo. "It will be a good night's pickings!"

Sure enough, EVERYBODY was at the party, and everybody wore top hats.

From backstage
Zoldo, Fred
and Ginger
kept a
look-out.

In a borrowed hat, Zoldo the Magnificent
stepped on to the stage. The crowd
applauded wildly. But Milo Drumgooey
took no notice of Zoldo.

The jewel thief began to thread very slowly among the crowd. Every time he saw some jewels he fancied, he would sneak up, whisper "Abracadabra", and the valuables would vanish. Seconds later they would reappear . . . in Milo's den.

Up on the stage Zoldo was half-way through his act when there was a small commotion at the back of the hall.

This was the moment they had been waiting for. Zoldo raised his hands. In one he held a magic wand.

"Ladies and gentlemen," he announced, "please stay exactly where you are. I am about to perform a brand new trick."

Everybody turned. Even Milo Drumgooey. Zoldo stepped off the stage and began to walk around the room. He passed from hat to hat. As he passed, he would say "excuse me". Then he would tap the hat, and call out "Abracadabra, ice-cream sundae!"

Pretty baffling, huh?

Milo Drumgooey was especially

baffled. He began to shuffle towards one of the fire exits. But it was too late. Just as he was reaching the edge of the crowd a familiar voice said: "Excuse me".

Before Milo could reply, or run, there was a tap on his hat, and Zoldo called out:

"Abracadabra, ice-cream sundae!"

Now, of course, if Milo had been wearing an ordinary hat, nothing would have happened. But this, as we know, was no ordinary hat!

There was a strange, muffled, squelching sound and Milo began to feel an uncomfortably squidgy feeling around his bald patch. A dribble of something cold and sticky slid down the back of his neck. The wand waved again.

"Custard!" yelled Zoldo. There was a

burbling, and the hat seemed to wobble and lift a little, as a yellow blob of custard lolloped down

on

to

Milo's

nose.

"Any requests?" Zoldo cried to the crowd. "Cola!" "Cheesecake!" "Banana split!"

"Milkshake!"

The wand waved and the hat

burbled and **burped**

and

blooped

and

hisssssssed

and

wobbled

and rose . . .

rose . . .

rose majestically upwards.

By the time the crowd had run

out of ideas Milo stood, quivering and

humiliated, with a mountain of melting

71

puddings subsiding gently down his face.

Zoldo stepped forward and carefully removed his stolen top hat from the mess that was Milo. "I do believe," he said, "that this is *my* hat!"

The crowd went wild with applause.

"And for my next trick . . ." Zoldo announced. He waved his wand over the upturned hat and muttered a special magic spell, taught to him by the Hat Man all those years ago.

Suddenly the hat was overflowing,
spilling a glittering cascade of valuables
on to the dance floor.

There were gasps as
watches and wallets and
earrings and rings came tumbling out.
Everybody began to cheer and clap
and shout "Encore! Encore!"

Everybody, that is, except Milo. He
was too busy . . .

ELEVEN

Next morning, Zoldo the Magnificent
became plain Windrush Gussett again.
His holiday plans had changed a bit
though. The hotel manager, overjoyed
that everyone's valuables had been
returned, insisted that Windrush should
move into the VIP suite and get five star
luxury treatment. As for Fred and

Ginger, they got positively chubby on
top grade bird seed.

For the rest of the holiday they all put
their feet up, relaxed in the sunshine and
completely forgot about magic.

I know what you're thinking.

You're thinking: "Hang about. What
happened to Milo Drumgooey and
Fang?"

Well, Milo Drumgooey and Fang managed to slip out of the party while Zoldo was returning valuables, and just as soon as Milo had washed all the goo out of his hair, they made their escape from the island.

They pedalled for all they were worth –
which wasn't much.

And if Zoldo has seen hide or hair of
either of them since . . .

he's
keeping
it
under
his
hat!